BE BRAVE, DO IT AFRAID!

By Nicole Minard

Illustration by Daisyblue Publishing

What is fear?

But just holding you back.

I'm afraid of this,
I'm afraid of all that.

This one **looks scary!**
And that one's too dark.

Sometimes **I pause,**

While others **just start.**

I see them **going around** with such fun.

I want to **go play!**
Before they are done.

I don't want to go home without
trying new things,
But when I get ready,
My tummy turns,
And says NO... NO... NO... please!

But I have to learn...
TO DO IT AFRAID.

Deep breath... I CAN DO THIS!
I can be BRAVE!

13

14

Oh wow! This is fun!
More fun than I thought.

First, I didn't want to,
And now I want to a lot.

I CAN learn...
TO DO IT AFRAID.

Deep breath...
I CAN DO THIS!
I can be BRAVE!

WHEE this is great!
WOW, that was good.

Fear wasn't holding me
as tight as it could.

And now
I am laughing and
having such fun,

To think,
I could have
missed out on this one.

Somethings I try,
I don't like it at all.

But sometimes... it's great!
Even if I do fall.

Anytime I get worried and
think 'I don't want to',

I remember something,
that I can cling to.

The thing that I've learned is...
TO DO IT AFRAID.

Deep breath...
I CAN DO THIS!

I can be BRAVE!

Keep going... keep trying...
JUST DO IT AFRAID.

Remember... deep breath...
YOU can do this!

You too can be BRAVE.

About the Author

Nicole Minard is a Behavior Analyst and mother dedicated to enriching the parenting experience through her Living Full Well collection. With her expertise in child development and Applied Behavior Analysis, Nicole crafts resources that blend practical parenting guides with positive affirmation stories to empower both children and parents. Her work promotes confidence, resilience, and the joy of parenting, aiming to help families navigate their journey with ease and happiness. Founder of a Behavior Analysis agency and co-founder of a babysitting organization, Nicole is committed to creating supportive environments for families which promote loving childhoods. Discover more about the collection and connect with Nicole at LivingFullWell.com and on Instagram to explore how each day of parenting can be a celebration.

Made in United States
Orlando, FL
13 December 2024

55618682R00020